MAXIM BILLER

INSIDE THE HEAD OF BRUNO SCHULZ

Translated from the German
by Anthea Bell

With two stories by Bruno Schulz

PUSHKIN PRESS
LONDON

Pushkin Press
71–75 Shelton Street, London WC2H 9JQ

Inside the Head of Bruno Schulz by Maxim Biller was
originally published in Germany as *Im Kopf von Bruno Schulz*
© 2013, Verlag Kiepenheuer & Witsch, Cologne

'Birds' and 'Cinnamon Shops' from *The Street of Crocodiles* by
Bruno Schulz, © C. J. Schulz 1963, © Jakob Schulz 1977, 1978.
Originally published in Polish as *Sklepy cynamonowe*, 1934.
Translated from the Polish by Celina Wieniewska, first
published by Walker and Company in 1963. Reproduced
with the kind permission of Bloomsbury Publishing Inc.

English translation © 2015 Anthea Bell

This translation first published by Pushkin Press in 2015

0 0 1

ISBN 978 1 782271 00 0

Frontispiece: Maxim Biller © Lottermann and Fuentes

Set in 10 on 13.5 Monotype Baskerville by Tetragon, London

Proudly printed and bound in Great Britain by TJ International,
Padstow, Cornwall on Munken Premium White 90gsm

www.pushkinpress.com

CONTENTS

INSIDE THE
HEAD OF
BRUNO SCHULZ

Praise be to him who creates strange beings.

S. Y. AGNON,
And the Crooked Shall Be Made Straight

"MY HIGHLY ESTEEMED, greatly respected, dear Herr Thomas Mann," wrote a small, thin, serious man slowly and carefully in his notebook, on a surprisingly warm autumn day in November 1938—and immediately crossed the sentence out again. He rose from the low, softly squealing swivel chair, where he had been sitting since early that afternoon at the desk, also too low, from his father's old office, he swung his arms upward and sideways a couple of times as if doing morning exercises, and looked for two or three minutes at the narrow, dirty, skylight panes of the top of the window, through which shoes and legs kept appearing, along with the umbrella tips and skirt hems of passers-by up above in Florianska Street. Then he sat down once more and began again.

"My dear sir," he wrote. "I know that you receive many letters every day, and probably spend more time answering them than writing your wonderful, world-famous novels. I can imagine what that means! I myself have to spend thirty-six hours a week teaching drawing to my beloved but totally untalented boys, and when, at the end of the day, I leave the Jagiełło High School where I am employed, tired and—". Here he broke off, stood up again, and as he did so knocked the desk with his left knee. However, instead of rubbing the injured knee, or hopping about the small basement room, cursing quietly, he held his head firmly with both hands—it was a very large, almost triangular, handsome head, reminiscent from a distance of those paper kites that his school students had been flying in the Koszmarsko stone quarry since the first windy days of September—and soon afterwards he let go of his head again with a single vigorous movement, as if that could help him to get his thoughts out. It worked, as it almost always did, and then he sat down at the desk again, took a fresh sheet of paper and wrote, quickly and without previous thought: "My dear Dr Thomas Mann! Although we are not personally acquainted, I must tell you that three weeks ago a German came to our town, claiming to be you. As I, like all of us in Drohobycz, know you only from newspaper photographs, I cannot say with complete certainty that he is not you, but the stories he tells alone—not to mention his shabby clothing and his strong body odor—arouse my suspicions."

Right, very good, that will do for the opening, thought the small, serious man in the basement of the Florianska Street building, satisfied, and he put his pencil—it was a Koh-i-Noor HB, and you could also draw with it if necessary—into the inside pocket of the thick Belgian jacket that he wore all year round. Then he closed the black notebook with the blank label at its first page, and stroked his face as if it did not belong to him. For the first time that day—no, for the first time in many months, maybe even years—he no longer felt that large black lizards and squinting snakes, as green as kerosene and with evil grins, were about to slither out of the walls around him; he did not hear the beating and rushing of gigantic *Archaeopteryx* wings behind him, as he usually did every few minutes; he was not afraid that soon, very soon indeed, something unimaginably dreadful was going to happen. When he realized that, he was immediately panic-stricken, for it must be a trap set for him by Fate.

Ever since he could remember Bruno—for that was the name of the man with the face like a paper kite—had awoken every morning with Fear in his heart. Fear and he had breakfast together in Lisowski's tearoom, Fear accompanied him to the High School and looked over his shoulder as the boys put their unsuccessful sketches of animals down in front of him, as well as plaster models, covered with black fingerprints, of their sweet little heads. Fear was there when he talked to other teachers during the break periods—their conversation was generally about the boys' unimportant bragging and misdeeds, or a new production at the Kaminski Theater in Warsaw, they hardly ever mentioned all the fuss the Germans were kicking up these days—and Fear did not leave him even when Helena Jakubowicz, the young sports and philosophy teacher, asked him how his new novel was getting on. Everyone in Poland who understood the first thing about literature, she said, was waiting for it with increasing impatience and interest. Only when Helena Jakubowicz—small, athletic and with a hairy face like a clever female bonobo chimpanzee—put her hand on his arm and pressed it did Fear go away. But as soon as Helena let go, Fear was back, and so he had to take it away with him to the large, darkened apartment in Stryj Street, where fortunately Fear did not follow him all the way into one of the girls' rooms. But as soon as he was outside again, Fear settled firmly down in his belly—which indeed was its favorite place—sat there like a large, hot, gray lump turning and rustling all the time, and he took it home with him. And then, even if after a brief supper, and after leafing through the *Tygodnik Ilustrowany* and the *Neue Freie Presse*, he was finally sitting at his father's old desk in the basement, Fear was there as well. Fear was with him as he wrote, as he drew, as he thought—and he always thought while he worked—of Papa's shrinking, dying body, or of the baffled way the Russian soldiers shook their heads when, in the second year of the war, they had accidentally set the Schulz family's house in the market place on fire. And when Fear felt tired and was going to slink away, he quickly imagined that it was he, not his mortally sick brother-in-law Jankel, who had felt impelled to cut his throat with a razor blade one cool summer morning—whereupon the gray lump began boring an even deeper hole in his belly. Only in his sleep was Bruno really alone. Then he dreamt of Zürich, Paris and New York, where there were hundreds and indeed thousands of ruined, thin-skinned people like him, smiling and waving at one another in cafés, parks and libraries, encouraging each other by means of slight, silent nods.

"Professor Schulz." Bruno suddenly heard a deep, but still uncertain boy's voice calling to him—a voice on the verge of breaking. "You weren't in school today! You'll get bad marks!" The boy laughed, and some of the other boys joined in. Then the boy knocked on the skylight with a stick, but it was more like the sound of a bird's beak, and the knocking, at first a soft, scraping sound, quickly grew louder. Bruno slipped off his chair onto the floor behind the desk, he took his head in his hands again, elbows propped wide apart, covered those big ears of his with his small hands, and as he briefly looked up at the skylight over the edge of the desk, he saw several small beaks scratching and pecking at the dirty glass. He immediately slid to the floor again, covered his ears even more firmly, and lost himself in the sound of the sea as the breaking waves ran in and out, a sound that spread from the middle of his head all over the world.

Bruno had really been hoping that no one in school would notice his absence, particularly not pretty Helena, whose thick, blonde and often badly combed hair unfortunately gave off the pungent smell of an animal cage, a mixture of urine and damp hay that had been left lying around. Yesterday she had shut him up, for almost a whole hour's lesson and without any light on, in the little room containing broken gymnastics equipment next to the sports hall. He didn't know why, but probably because he had trembled even more than usual during their last conversation in a break period, and couldn't be soothed even by the pressure of her short, but sharp and unfiled fingernails. So what? She shouldn't have asked him to let her see at least a few pages of his novel, and he had been cold as well, in spite of the summery days that came like a gift in mid-November, and in spite of the fact that he was wearing his heavy jacket. When she finally let him out he was feeling very much better, or so he told her at least, for fear of making her even angrier, and she promised to shut him up again sometime soon. Maybe, she added, she'd come into the little room with him herself for a while if he liked. She could go to one of the chaotic shops beyond the market place that opened only late in the evening for a few hours, sometimes not even that, and buy some things that she'd been wanting to try out with him for a long time. He could guess what she meant! No, he had replied, he'd rather she didn't, although he immediately felt very safe and well at the thought of those things—black leather Venetian Columbine masks stuffed with sawdust; penis-sized Pierrots made of willow rods, and Easter whips interwoven with thin steel chains; silver nipple clamps, and Japanese shunga candles (their dripping wax left no blisters behind on the skin). He wondered, even as he hurried up to the second floor and his class of shouting boys in the art room, whether to say he was sick next day. Then, when he was on his way home, it occurred to him that he had been meaning for a long time to write to Thomas Mann in Zürich, and that decided the matter: he would be off school sick tomorrow!

"The way the alleged Thomas Mann eats and speaks is also suspicious," Bruno wrote in his notebook now, still sitting on the floor, while the tapping on the window pane died down. "It is true that he cuts up the meat and potatoes on his plate in a bored manner, just like a surgeon studying his patient's tissue, first spreading the napkin on his lap even more lovingly than stern Adele used to place freshly shaken-out quilts and pillows on our beds. But then the stranger will suddenly fling his knife and fork wildly across the restaurant in the Swaying Pyramid Hotel, where he has occupied the manager Hasenmass's bathroom for weeks, he seizes the food on his plate with his hands, stuffs it into his mouth, and blood spurts all over his shirt and into his eyes. Fortunately, he has not yet hit anyone with the flying cutlery! All the important people in our town, who have been hovering around him since his arrival like a colony of bees around their queen, duck for a moment and then come up again—the corners of their mouths stretched in a subservient smile, their eyes glazed and reddened with alarm—and ask him please to go on telling them his exciting stories."

Bruno paused for a moment. The unpleasant tapping and scraping of the birds' beaks had stopped, but now evening, almost night had fallen, as abruptly and menacingly as it did every day of his life. In the basement, however, stale twilight still reigned, with the remnants of many terrible and futile hours of work, and that immediately reminded him yet again of the fact that, so far, only the title existed of the great book that he had been promising his friends, his colleagues, and the women he knew in Lemberg, Warsaw and here at home for years—not a page, not a drawing. He didn't even know what the book was going to be about. At least he had finally written his first story in German, and if, with the aid of Thomas Mann, it were to appear in the *Neuer Rundschau* or in the *Sammlung*, not even his fear could keep him from leaving Drohobycz and Poland for ever. A friendly letter from the famous writer in reply to his, a recommendation from him to the publishing houses of Querido in Amsterdam or Bermann Fischer in Stockholm, and he would throw a couple of manuscripts, his drawing pads, some underwear and his shaving things into Papa's old leather suitcase and set off for freedom.

"The longer the stranger stays here," Bruno continued his letter, while a high-spirited smile brightened his stern, almost sad face, "the more often he is asked what has brought him, the famous winner of the Nobel Prize, to a little backwater like Drohobycz. Have his works not been translated into thirty-seven languages? Doesn't he count Albert Einstein, Arthur Rubinstein and Franklin D. Roosevelt among his friends? Isn't he more prosperous than all the Polish and Yiddish writers of West Galicia put together, and couldn't he therefore, if he were coming to our part of the world, afford to stay in a suite at the Russischer Hof hotel? He always gives a different answer—either with exaggerated friendliness, or angrily stamping his muddy walking shoes, which are full of holes. Sometimes he says that he is no longer safe in Zürich, because the Germans have begun throwing their enemies out of the windows of houses in secret, but they would certainly never come to Poland. Sometimes he mentions a terribly deformed yet very sociable Lithuanian-American businessman who has lived in Drohobycz for years, and who could get him, his wife and his six children a visa to go to the States. I have never heard of this Mr Katanauskas before, and even the members of our friendly Thomas Mann Committee don't know him, but of course they dare not question the master more closely."

Bruno paused again, and not knowing how to go on he raised his eyes in the search for inspiration. In the twilight of the basement he did not recognize his own drawings, which covered all the walls and, because of the constant damp down there, were as wrinkled as old women's skin. In the faint light of evening, the bodies and faces of the men, women, birds, horses and dogs that Bruno could never stop drawing looked even more distorted, translucent and vulnerable; they seemed to be simultaneously living and dead, and that gave him a new idea.

"One evening," he went on, after skimming what he had already written and correcting two or three passages, "the alleged Thomas Mann also told us, in the bar of the Swaying Pyramid, that he wanted to collect material for his next novella here in the town of the

Jagienka-Łomska pogrom. The novella, he said with an almost sadistic chuckle, would be about the abduction and murder of a little Christian girl, just as it was in the real pogrom. Suspicion—and he couldn't stop laughing, dear Dr Mann, while striking the manager Hasenmass several times on his bald patch—suspicion would fall first on her own uncle, then on the Jews of the town, and because it soon became clear that the uncle was indeed the guilty party, the Christians were in such a rage that they killed the Jews and set fire to their houses. Then, when the fire spread to their own quarter of Drohobycz, they accused one another of destroying the town, fell upon each other and fought with knives and pitchforks, raped their best friends, both men and women, and their children and mothers. 'Well, my friends,' said the false stranger to us when he had finished, and was wiping tears of laughter from his eyes, 'how do you like this story? How would you reply to the question of guilt that I am about to ask? I would say: if the Hebrews had never come to Drohobycz, that pointless and utterly destructive pogrom would never have taken place, would it?' Then he beat a short but vigorous drum roll on the manager's head with the palms of both his hands."

There was another knock, this time at the closed basement door and much louder, but also more amiable than the idiotic, petty noise that his students had kicked up earlier with their beaks and claws. Bruno, crouching on the floor once again, this time on all fours, with his open notebook in front of him like a dog with its beloved bone, shook himself and tried to get a word out of his throat. But he could utter only a growl, for he was concentrating too hard, as he did whenever he was writing a story. "Brunio," he heard his sister Hania calling from outside, "someone telephoned you. Are you in there? What's that terrible noise?"

"Who telephoned?" he replied, with difficulty.

"Someone from the school."

"What, so late?"

"Why ask me?"

"Was it a… a woman or a man?"

"A woman."

"At eight in the evening."

Hania said nothing, and he thought: she's only making that up. Ever since, ten years ago, he had found the mortally sick Jankel with his throat cut and his limbs outstretched on the lounger in the back garden, her imagination had flourished like the gigantic black rose in his *Treatise on Tailors' Dummies*. For instance, a day after shloshim, the period of mourning, she had told him that Jankel wasn't dead, they had buried the wrong man, an acquaintance of Adele's had seen him twice in Warsaw. Adele was also the source of another of Hania's stories. Apparently, Hania had told him a couple of months ago, now that Adele could no longer preside over her house and the souls in it, she had set up in business in Stryj Street, and there she was often visited by a man who—apparently—looked remarkably like Hania's small, timid hypochondriac of a brother Bruno. However, he couldn't be Bruno, because he examined the half-naked girls like a horse dealer, drank a lot of wine, and told dirty jokes. Why did Hania tell stories that got on his nerves like that? What made her think of them? He had never seen Adele in Stryj Street, Hania was simply making it up so that he would feel as confused and insecure as she did. When they talked politics it was just the same. When he explained to Hania that the Germans' appetite for Danzig and Upper Silesia would never be greater than their fear of Poland's allies England and France, his sister, whose wits had been turned by her husband's suicide, looked at him as if he were deranged. She stroked his head and whispered that in the next war more than just their own house would be burnt down—that was as certain as the destruction of the Second Temple, and she hoped there would be more left of her and him, and the children and Jankel than a few ashes and what Bruno had written about them in his two books.

"What did the woman want, Hania?" said Bruno slowly and crossly, for he wanted to go on writing quickly, and he thought: good, at least talking works again.

"She said you weren't in school today, and in your absence your students had destroyed the stuffed animals in the art room and thrown them into the light-well of the yard," Hania called through the door in her high, faded, widow's voice. "And she said that was why you were to look in today and take your punishment. If you didn't, she said, it would be worse tomorrow. Will you eat with us first, Brunio? Jankel is in Lemberg until Tuesday, and I have more than enough meat and kreplach." She sighed. "You know, even if he's only away for a day or two on business I miss him as if he were never coming back. We eat at nine!"

As you see, my greatly respected Herr Thomas Mann, thought Bruno, your double is not the only person in Drohobycz who has lost his wits. It began early with my sister Hania, and my father was in even more of a hurry to leave the world. Long before his death, he resorted to that in-between realm where, he thought, human beings, animals and plants could communicate without words. Shaking his head, Bruno put the black notebook aside, laid the pencil on the ice-cold floor, where it quickly rolled away like a frightened mouse, stopped when it reached one of the legs of the desk and stayed there. As my beloved and now dead mother nursed him, thought Bruno, without noticing that he was no longer writing, she, too, discovered the joys of unreality. To her way of thinking my father—even when he was as small as a baby again, lying in our little dog Nimrod's basket, weeping and whispering as he nestled against the baffled animal—was a guilty man exploiting his mortal sickness to avoid responsibility for his house and his family, and so she would some-times throw things at him: the key to the front door, or her *siddur* prayer book when she was in the middle of praying. Ever since then, my dear Herr Mann, I have asked myself three times a day: did Mama learn that from our implacable jailer Adele? Did she know how often Adele—a tiny woman, but often endowed by her fury with superhuman strength—had raised her hand to me in the old days, in one of the forgotten, empty, dusty attic rooms in our old house on the market place? I think there can be no two answers to that question. Once the roughly made wooden door of one of the rooms, where I was in the middle of my little conversation with Adele's feather duster as it whistled through the air, was left open, and when I turned my head aside in pain I saw Mama's helpless, harlequin face in the gap where the door stood ajar. Do you see what kind of a madhouse this town of Drohobycz is now, Dr Mann? People here never think and act as they should! I could tell you so many tales: my students, instead of drawing and doing their arithmetic exercises, generally perch on the rooftops of the houses, cooing and pecking, or fly in circles around the tower of the town hall. Hasenmass the hotel manager—I saw this through the window late at night last Saturday—has himself harnessed to a hackney cab by your double, and, naked and whinnying softly, he takes the master from bar to bar. Perelmann, the under-age, melancholy editor-in-chief of the *Drohobycz News*, writes every day in his paper that the Jews ought to renounce their faith, as they once did overnight in Spain in the past, and then they would soon be leading Torquemada's divisions instead of being crushed by them. And Dr Franck, the specialist in internal medicine, closed his practice last month and sits on a bench at the railway station all day, reciting the *Kaddish* all the time.

And what about the lovely, gloomy Helena Jakubowicz? She, poor woman, believing too much in the enlightening power of literature and ideas, suffers from particularly severe depression, the result, as one tells oneself, of extreme literary ambition accompanied by only average talent. I do not know what it is that she likes about my stories. She takes them, she has told me a couple of times, as you might take an aspirin or, no, an antidote to the poison of hopelessness within herself. And having to wait so long for my new book often makes her even sadder—hence her eternal, abnormal, wild and illogical anger with me, the compliant scapegoat, the anger that comforts me whenever I am not holding Helena in check, and gives me the reassuring knowledge that childhood, snow-white or blood-red, will never pass away and become happiness. It really is a shame, Herr Mann, that you will never meet Helena. What a delicate, dear woman is hidden in reality behind the ill-smelling, downy, monkey hair on her face! And what if she were to wash and comb her hair properly for once, if she were to remove the sticky sawdust from her hair and her clothes, if she were to have a pedicure and put on a pretty, close-fitting French skirt suit? Then, ah then, I fear that perhaps I would never tremble with such pleasant desire in her presence. Now you can see how crazy a man gets to be if he lives here too long.

"I am not hungry, Hania," said Bruno slowly and indistinctly, as if awakening from a deep sleep. Once again that growl came out of his throat, but this time it did not alarm him. "I am going to do a little more work, and later look in at the High School to see what they want me for there. Don't wait for me." He tried to stand up as quietly as possible, so as not to make any noise that would start Hania talking again, but she had already gone upstairs, for he heard her now in the kitchen above him playing a wild military march on pans, plates and the oven. At first his attempt to stand up went well. Bruno raised his torso and kept his balance without having to support himself with his hands on the cold stone floor—but when he tried getting to his feet he tottered, and had to kneel down again at once. He stayed like that for minutes on end, surprised to find that today, of all days, he had lost the ability to stand upright and walk. For many years he had expected that to happen, but not now, not until much later—in a future endlessly far away, populated by gigantic wall lizards, snakes and primeval birds who ate their own tails, by armies of human beings in gray uniforms in long, straggling processions that reached to the horizon, by millions of naked men, women and children who could move only on all fours. And everywhere in that country, fires large and small were burning, and anyone who could see through the smoke and the flames shooting up around him prayed that he might not be forced, like those people, to his hands and knees, and be driven like them into that fire.

"Professor! Professor! Don't be afraid, we'll see you safely through town to the High School! Mrs Jakubowicz isn't as angry with you as you think, we've been talking to her about you. And she forgave us at once."

Had he dreamt it, or had his students just called that out to him in chorus—cheeping, chirping, clear as a bell—from outside the skylight which was suddenly half open, flapping quietly in the wind? Bruno, still crouching on the floor with his head leaning on the greasy brown seat of the chair, acted as if he hadn't heard anything. For some time, lying in wait like a cat with his eyes narrowed, he watched the pencil that had rolled away, and then suddenly snatched it up.

"It seems to me," he wrote in his notebook again, pressing it open against the desk drawer, which stood ajar, "as if the people of Drohobycz had been waiting for someone like the false winner of the Nobel Prize to come to their town and turn their heads even more, my dear and highly esteemed Dr Mann. They have been living for too long with no contact with the outside world, a provincial existence makes them anxious, crazy, curious. They plan a day's excursion to Stryj months in advance, and before anyone here travels to the capital, he visits Reynisz the notary to put his affairs in order. You should see the people of Drohobycz for yourself! They almost all have attractive, pale, friendly faces, behind which they conceal either nothing at all—or the longing for eternal bright nights and a pain that is otherwise described only in history books. I know"—he hesitated, but then quickly went on writing—"I know what I am talking about, for I am no exception. I have studied in Vienna and Lemberg, and all the same I came back again. I had a fiancée whose name I often forget; she left me because for years I promised to move to live with her in Warsaw, without ever really meaning it. And when I was awarded the Golden Laurel of the Academy of Literature last month, I lay in bed for days weeping, instead of being glad. So I too, my most esteemed Dr Mann, have recently let your double deceive me like everyone else. Last Saturday, when he was going down Florianska Street drawn along by Hasenmass the hotel manager, I did not just cast a quick glance out of the window and then quickly return to my work. Oh no! I leapt up from my desk, I tore off my clothes as I ran, and when I had caught up with the cab in which your ill-omened double sat, stiff and haughty as a German professor, I let myself be harnessed to it too as I went on full speed ahead, and so we trotted away to the Swaying Pyramid Hotel on the market place. Once we had arrived we were permitted (without the carriage, of course, but in full harness) to accompany the master into the manager's bathroom, where he has been staying since his arrival in Drohobycz. This bathroom—it is almost as large as the hall of the Jagiełło High School, and I hope you have comparable rooms in your new house in Zürich—contained no washbasins, no lavatory, no bathtub, only several showers fitted into the bare concrete ceiling, two benches and a long rail with clothes-hooks hanging from it. Obviously the false Nobel Prize winner had had everything removed as soon as he moved in, to leave more space for his many visitors. Those present that night were: Mrs Hasenmass; Lisowski the baker, with his wife and three sons; Adele; almost all my students; Mr Perelmann and Helena Jakubowicz; Jankel, my sister's late husband; Reynisz the notary; and my friend and colleague Czarski, editor-in-chief of the *Tygodnik Ilustrowany*, who was staying in Drohobycz in order to persuade me (of course in vain) to publish a fragment of my novel in his journal. Later we were joined by a man whom I did not know, an American with half his face covered by a sparkling metal mask. This was the mysterious Mr Katanauskas. They had all"—here Bruno looked up and, before writing on, studied the large drawing on the wall to the right of the door, which depicted half a dozen small, thin, naked men kneeling in front of a young lady in high-heeled shoes and a torn ball gown, with their avid eyes, full of despair and desire, open wide as if they were slowly suffocating under the influence of an invisible opiate—"they had all, like me and Hasenmass the hotel manager, stripped naked. They had hung their clothes on the hooks, and they sat in silence, or engaged in excessively low-voiced conversation with each other, on the two benches, waiting. When the master entered, with the hotel manager and me, they rose at almost the same time, covered their bare chests and their genitals with their hands, and even the last and quietest conversations died down. The false Thomas Mann at first acted as if the over-intimate and pushy behavior of his guests, if one may so call it, was unwelcome to him. As they suddenly began moving towards him, like a brood of turtles slowly awakening and making their way from the beach into the water, he raised his hands in a gesture of rejection. He briskly twirled the ends of his mustache, then took a half-smoked cigar from the inside pocket of his shabby tweed jacket, which was buttoned up the wrong way, and tried to light it. He succeeded only at the third or fourth attempt. 'How are you, my friends?' he said uncertainly, and the cigar smoke that he puffed out mingled with his breath, which smelt of something rotten. 'I'm glad to see you again. I'm afraid I must return to Zürich tomorrow to fetch my wife and children. After that we shall board a train for Marseilles, and we go on from there by sea to New York. We have the prospect of a very pretty villa in Princeton; I think I shall be able to pay for it cash down with the advances for the last part of the *Joseph* tetralogy. I'm very sorry that I must leave you here alone; I know the times will get no better, and the guarantees of the Allies are, as we can see from the example of the poor Czechs and Slovaks, worth nothing. But good Mr Katanauskas has kept his promise, and we can set off for America at last. We would be stupid not to go, don't you agree?' They all—as one man—took a stride towards him, and then another stride and yet another, they murmured softly, 'Oh dear' and 'Please don't go', and the first arms were already winding around his throat and his arms. 'It's not my fault, believe me,' he said, 'please stop this, it's uncomfortable for me. Stop it!' By now the manager Hasenmass's bathroom was full of metallic blue smoke, and you could hardly see whose hand was tugging at the alleged Thomas Mann's hair, which was slicked back with gel, while he tried to unbutton his shirt. 'Stop that at once!' he cried again. Then he produced, as if from nowhere, the horsewhip that he had never once had to use during our harmonious ride through the sleeping town of Drohobycz, and he began fending off the naked men who were pestering him with short, sharp cracks of that whip. I myself—I was standing beside that twitching, sighing, ever-growing human pyramid as it collapsed on itself—I myself, unfortunately, was struck by none of them. He whipped the men, then the women, then even the children, and if there had still been traces of reluctance to be seen at first in his long, masterful and treacherous face, as it kept emerging in the hazy cigar smoke, he seemed to be coming to enjoy all this whipping, pushing and cursing. 'Is it my fault that a decent man like me can't be sure of his life in Europe today?' he exclaimed, striking the weeping editor-in-chief Perelmann a blow on the nose with the handle of the whip. 'I'd rather be at home in Munich watching little boys in Briennerstrasse than wading in the swamps of Galicia!' he cried, bela-boring the buttocks of the sighing Adele. Then he turned to the totally confused baker Lisowski, who had probably last read more than three consecutive sentences at his bar-mitzvah ceremony, and while he covered the baker's fat belly and upper arms with red welts from the whip he cried, 'You and those bandits in Berlin are to blame for everything that's going wrong: Germany, Europe, the world. You were the first to say that humanity is alone, and so now every other idiot takes himself for God on earth!' Yes, my highly esteemed Dr Mann, even Mr Katanauskas"—and the same rigid smile with which his students sometimes adorned the kites flying over the Koszmarsko stone quarry appeared on Bruno's face—"even he was not spared. Only now he was crying in his fine Vilna Yiddish that he wanted to go to New York with you, one pogrom in his life was enough, and as honorary American consul he had the same rights as those he was helping—when he got a push in his bare belly from your double, and as he fell his metal mask was kicked. The mask came off, landed clinking and dancing on the floor, and now, in so far as it was possible to see it in the smoke wafting back and forth, a half-burnt face with a dark, empty eye socket came into view. Then it was poor Helena's turn, and after her came my students, who at some point, instead of fluttering about Hasenmass's bathroom screeching, formed a protective circle around their gasping and exhausted teacher Helena with wings spread wide. But gradually the blows inflicted by the German grew weaker, and so did his voice, in the silvery clouds of smoke the wavering contours of the sad, childish face of Lieutenant Alfred Dreyfus formed for a moment, then the French officer became the weeping, bleeding Jagienka Łomska, then I saw myself coming out of the smoke, and finally the cloud turned, coalesced and climbed to the ceiling, where it disappeared with a loud hiss into the jets of the showers—thus revealing a great heap of naked bodies lying lifeless around the false Thomas Mann as he knelt there, exhausted. 'Me too,' I cried in all the confusion. 'I want to come too!' But as he mopped the sweat off his throat and forehead with a handkerchief that was stiff and sticky with dirt, he replied in a friendly tone, 'Not you, you'll still be needed. You must write your novel. What is it to be called? *The Messiah*, am I right? To work, get down to work, and when you have finished those bandits will come from Berlin to your little town and burn you along with your wonderful manuscript. Too bad—it's your own fault!' He laughed. 'Terrific, what a subject! But who will write a novel about it when you are dead, Jew Schulz?'"

Maybe the ending goes a little too far, thought Bruno, as he read the last pages of his letter to his famous and influential colleague in Zürich. Will he believe it of me? Will he give me his support? Won't he think I mean him? And suddenly his companion Fear was back, Fear who had left him for the last couple of hours, and the hot gray lump was turning in his belly again. At the same time Hania's loud footsteps shook the black and now almost invisible basement ceiling from above, and he was afraid that she might at any moment break through the floor of the kitchen with her high stiletto heels and pierce his head. Hania—poor, intolerable Hania—had recently taken to wearing her expensive French shoes even at home, as well as her chiffon dress from Lunarski & Klein in Warsaw, for she was expecting the late Jankel back anytime soon, and wanted to be beautiful for him. And as she almost never took off the dress, not even when she was cooking, and certainly not now, it was covered with splashes of red borscht and dried yellow bits of dough, and its lovely white puff sleeves had dozens of holes burnt in them. Hania was not the only bundle of nerves in the house. Her two sons were also getting more and more restless from week to week, and were in a bad way. Their trousers and shirts were torn, they had dark red, almost black scabs on their bare knees, they cut each other's unwashed hair with the kitchen scissors, so that it looked untidy and all tousled as if they were vagrants, and Bruno hadn't seen them in school for months. When their mother asked them something, they either didn't reply at all, or threatened to throw her out of the house, so she generally kept quiet in their presence. However, Jacek and Chaimele left their uncle in peace. Only sometimes, when he was lying on Papa's old, greasy, Biedermeier sofa with its huge vultures' feet and claws and, quietly moving his lips, read a book or drew a sketch, did they talk about him in whispers. "Who's going to look after us when the Russians or the Germans come?" Jacek said to Chaimele a few days ago. And Chaimele replied, giggling, "Uncle Bruno, of course. Along with the tarts from Stryj Street and his writer friends in Warsaw, he's sure to know what to do." Whereupon Bruno uttered a quiet whistle of alarm, gave the sofa a little pat, and it immediately pattered out of the living room with him and into the library, where he could be undisturbed again.

By now it was so dark in Bruno's basement study that he could hardly read his own handwriting. The faint, orange, fantastic light of the street lamps that had just come on outside in Florianska Street was lost halfway between the open skylight and his easel, where he had hung up his hat and coat for years, and sometimes he imagined hanging himself up on it. He quickly stood up, forced himself back behind the low desk and switched on the handsome, cold, German lamp, with its black metal shade that even after years shone like polished cavalry boots. Only when he was sitting on Papa's creaking old office chair did it occur to him that he was no longer crouching on the floor, like one of the creatures from his daydreams that had no will of their own, scribbling violet lines, squiggles and little hooks, like an insect, in his notebook, marks that might even make some kind of sense in the end. But Fear was still there, and Fear whispered: you must come to the point. Do you know how many letters he gets every day? Yes, I do, replied Bruno, but do you really think I can write to him now and tell him what I really want him to do? Yes, why not, replied Fear, although I'm not perfectly sure, because I am Fear. Haven't I overdone it? said Bruno. I mean saying that someone else is pretending to be him, could be him, but that he is so brutish and arrogant to the very people who respect him and sing his praises. I mean, it does sound rather unlikely, doesn't it? Do you know the story of the people of Sichem, asked Fear, do you know what happened to them after they had chosen Abimelech as ruler of the Philistines? Not exactly, said Bruno, will you tell me? Later, maybe, said Fear, you're not ready for it yet.

"The day before yesterday, dear Dr Mann," Bruno went on writing quickly by the light of his German lamp, while he pressed the thumb and forefinger of his left hand to his temples, which were suddenly aching, "Dr Franck came to see me at the school. As you already know, he is the former specialist in internal medicine who no longer wants to submit to the laws of everyday life. Instead he sits at the railway station talking to himself, or he recites prayers and blessings out loud, all jumbled up—he of all people, the atheist and one of the first Zionists in our town. After knocking so quietly that you could hardly hear him, Dr Franck came into the art room and asked me to go out with him. At first the boys did not want to let me go—they never want to be left alone, you see, because then they always attack one another like enemies. When they began begging, tugging at my jacket with their beaks, Dr Franck—I had not seen him so clear and determined since he closed the practice—held his outstretched forefinger in front of his mouth and said a long, slow, 'Ssh!' At once they fell silent, and flew back to their places. Some of them went on drawing, some hid their heads under their wings and fell asleep."

Bruno stopped massaging his temples and, with his notepad close to his face, went over and brushed aside a few tiny gray and white feathers that had sunk slowly from above onto the paper. Instead of sinking to the floor they flew up into the vortex that had risen and performed a little dance in front of his flat, paper-kite nose. Bruno watched them, smiling, and kept blowing them up in the air again, then he lowered his head and wrote: "No sooner had Dr Franck and I closed the classroom door behind us than he began talking to me excitedly. It was about your double, Dr Mann. Of course he had not left Drohobycz after his nocturnal performance in the hotel manager Hasenmass's bathroom. He has never yet done what he said he would do. He explained that his wife had fallen sick in Zürich, and besides, he must wait for the rest of his library, which was stuck in Customs in a Reichsbahn railway car at the border near Basle, so he meant to make use of this extra time to stay in our town, working in peace before his great journey to America. Two days later he gave a reading in the pharmacy on the market place—he stood at the sales desk and, despite protests from the apothecary Hulciner, we had made ourselves comfortable in all the little drawers and compartments. Apparently he was reading the first pages of the continuation of his novel about the confidence trickster Felix Krull, but anyone can say that. It is true that what he read didn't sound bad—Krull decides to go to the circus, gets to know a rich and beautiful Englishwoman whom he does not love, and so on—but the sentences were trite and pompous. This evening it was finally clear to me that he cannot be the real Thomas Mann, for one thing because he appeared in a blood-red Persian robe, loosely tied with a curtain cord that had been pulled down, with his bare chest showing and a small, wildly twitching snake between his legs. And now Dr Franck was standing in the hall of the Jagiełło High School in front of me, telling me firmly, but with quivering lips, what he had seen and heard a few hours earlier. That morning the alleged Thomas Mann—his hair, which was usually combed smoothly back, tousled, rouge on his cheeks, his thin mustache shaved off and then painted on again with shoe cream—had been sitting next to him in a niche in the station cafeteria, talking in German to someone whom Dr Franck did not know. This other man had a high, squeaky, pleasing voice"— here Bruno stopped writing, closed his eyes and thought of a German movie actor whose dishonest, superior manner, reminiscent of Wilhelm Busch's naughty boys Max and Moritz, always drew comments in the form of loud whistles from the spectators in the Drohobycz

Palace Cinema—"and had the amiable and familiar face of a neighbor to whom you would entrust the key to your own apartment before going away on a journey. They were conversing in such low voices that at first Dr Franck could not hear what it was all about. He caught the word 'movement' once or twice, and the name of the Soviet Foreign Minister Molotov was also mentioned. Then the alleged Thomas Mann, speaking in a rather louder and more agitated voice than his companion (who wore a long, black, gleaming leather coat that rustled as he moved, and that he had not removed in the cafeteria), began enumerating the surnames of the Jewish inhabitants of Drohobycz. They kept laughing—particularly at those names that also had a literal meaning in German, such as Gottesdiener (servant of God), Katzenellenbogen (cat's elbow), Wahrhaftig (truthful), Hasenmass (hare's measure)—and finally the other man said it was all so witty, he really couldn't take any more of it, and he asked the false Thomas Mann to give him a written list of all the Jews in town instead, with their addresses and a brief assessment of their physical strength and financial circumstances. At some point"—and again little gray and white feathers fell from the air and settled on Bruno's notepad, he felt a not unpleasant breath of wind pass over him, now hot and now cold, and heard the soft tripping of small birds' feet coming closer from all sides—"at some point Dr Franck, who was finding the conversation of the two men increasingly sinister, closed his eyes, and he began reciting the *Shacharit* morning prayer for the eighth or tenth time that morning. But then his curiosity got the better of him, and he looked past the wooden partition between the tables in the cafeteria at the two Germans sitting there. Of course his eyes immediately met those of the man in the leather coat, who nodded to Dr Franck, without showing any surprise, pointed his forefinger at him like a commissioner on a Red Army poster and said, 'I like your people's prayers, and the *Shema Israel* is particularly fine. It would be a loss if there were no one left to recite it.' Do you understand now, Dr Mann, why I am writing to you?"

Bruno got to his feet in agitation, walked twice, then a third time around the desk, and when he sat down again there were two little doves perching on the lamp, one white and one gray, looking at him in silence. On the window sill above there were more doves, and some beside his chair as well, but he took no notice of this sudden plague of birds in his basement study.

"Dr Franck and I," he went on writing, pausing again and again, "are in no doubt, Dr Mann, of what is going on here: we are being spied on! Exactly what the Germans plan to do we do not know. We know only how the Jews are faring in their old home, and we hope that the new Nazi realm will not go on and on growing, to reach our town one day with its kraken arms. Dr Franck, who as President of the Poalei Zion movement in the old days would have liked to move the whole of Drohobycz to the banks of the Jordan or the mountains of Galilee, now says that if the enemies of the Jews begin to rage, there will be nothing left for us anyway but prayer. And he thinks we ought to continue remaining on good terms with your double, as it may help us later. So Dr Franck has also offered him his own apartment in Drohobycz for the rest of his stay here, because it is much lighter and more comfortable than the hotel manager's bathroom. After we had been standing together in silence for a little longer—while the noise made by the students went on in the art room—Dr Franck suddenly took my arm and asked me whether he could stay with us until the worst was over. What was I to reply? That Hania hates having guests? That the atmosphere on his bleak station bench is better than in our cold, sad house? That we are all lost anyway, and God has another end in view for every one of us?"

No sooner had Bruno written the last sentence than the warm gray lump in his belly became so hot that he had to take off his heavy tweed jacket and unbutton the collar of his shirt. He hung the jacket over the back of Papa's chair, and spent some time looking in silence at the two doves on his desk. Without moving, they looked back, also in silence. Then he carefully opened the lower compartment of his desk and took a large old cigar box out of it. He kept the things that were really important to him in this box: the tiny, well-worn brass hearing trumpet that Papa, in his last months of life, was always holding against the floor of the family's old house on the market place, so as to get a better idea of what the mice, spiders and martens living under it had to say. Adele's feather duster, of which he had both good and bad memories. And distributed everywhere in the cigar box was the sawdust, with its unpleasant odor, that he had secretly collected from the smelly, tangled hair of Helena Jakubowicz over the past years. Like someone digging for gold, he would run his fingers through that damp yellow pile of sawdust, thinking of the delightful and dangerous things that Helena Jakubowicz bought for the two of them in one of the badly lit shops that were always changing their location beyond the market place—and soon he felt reassured again and stopped sweating.

"Professor Schulz," the gray dove said to him, in the firm but still slightly pubertal voice of young Theo Rosenstock, staring at him out of small black eyes as if he were blind, "Mrs Jakubowicz has sent us again. She says you must hurry. She doesn't have much time, because afterwards she has a date to meet the gentleman from Germany in the Savoy Bar, and she also has to correct our philosophy essays by tomorrow."

"I'm sure to get top marks," said the white dove, giggling. Bruno recognized the girlish voice of Hermann, the baker Lisowski's middle son, who was as stupid as he was sweet, and he wished very much that the boy was right in what he said.

"Oh no, you won't," said the gray dove. "Hegel's *Phenomenology of Spirit*. What do you know about that?"

"Nothing," said the white dove. "But in the long break period I helped Mrs Jakubowicz to get all those flies and beetles out of her hair, and oh, how good they tasted!"

"Hermann, you're such a sweet little idiot," said the gray dove, nodding its head jerkily back and forth a few times, and plucking at its tousled breast feathers with its immaculate beak. The white dove imitated it, then they both laughed, the gray dove spread its wings, rose quickly in the air, turned two or three somersaults above the desk, and settled beside the other bird again on the black, shiny shade of Bruno's lamp. "And I'll get top marks at sport," said the dove. "Isn't that so, Professor? But I'll get a much lower mark for art, won't I?"

Bruno nodded. He carefully closed the cigar box and put it on the desk. Then he placed the pencil in his notebook, closed it and said, in the detached voice of someone talking in his sleep, "What does Mrs Jakubowicz want from me, Theo? Why must I go to the school so late this evening? I told them I was sick."

"You're to take your punishment, Professor," said the white dove.

"Be quiet!" the gray dove interrupted.

"I thought that Mrs Jakubowicz wasn't angry with me anymore. Were you lying to me just now, boys?"

Theo and Hermann did not reply, and the other doves who had gathered on the window sill and the floor abruptly stopped tripping back and forth, and looked in their direction quietly and in suspense.

"Punishment?" said Bruno. "What kind of punishment? What for?"

"Go on, Theo," said the white dove, "tell him. If you don't I will, but then I'm bound to get everything all muddled up. And then Mrs Jakubowicz will be angry with me and so will Professor Schulz."

Theo sailed down from the lamp to the table, perched on Bruno's hand, ran up the sleeve of his shirt, which was drenched with sweat, and settled on his shoulder. "But you must put your ear very close to me, Professor," he said, "because I'd rather tell you quietly."

Bruno did as his student asked, and then he heard a wild hissing and whistling deep in his ear. "She says," whispered Theo, gently touching Bruno's ear with his bony little beak again and again, "she says that you're infecting us all with your melancholy. She thinks you are more afraid than anyone she has ever met, and that means it is likely that you will refuse to let us have what would probably be the best books a human being could ever write. Your pessimism is really intolerable, she says, you are a bad, bad—"

At this moment someone drummed loudly on the

basement door. The doves—including Theo—flew up in alarm, and some of them hit their heads on the basement ceiling. They were all flapping their wings frantically, and the room was immediately full of a cloud of tiny gray, white and brown feathers, and an unbearable smell like a birdcage.

"Mama wants to know whether you're coming up to supper or not, Uncle Bruno," cried Chaimele and Jacek from outside, as if with a single voice. "Or do you have to go to Stryj Street today?" They laughed, and their laughter sounded like a wave rolling swiftly up and breaking several times—and then, without waiting for Bruno's answer, they ran noisily upstairs again. Seconds later, Bruno heard chairs being moved about in the kitchen above him, and the sound of knives and forks against Mama's old Russian porcelain plates.

"Keep quiet, children," said Bruno quietly to the doves, "and please don't disturb me. Sit down somewhere in peace and think of something nice, like what presents you would like for Chanukah or for your birthday. I have to finish writing a letter in a hurry, so that I can post it later on my way to the school. Yes, thank you, that's nice of you."

The birds immediately calmed down. Most of them settled beside the long, narrow window, which was black as night, and put their well-formed little heads under their wings, like good children. A few fluttered through the open skylight into the darkness, and Theo and Hermann, beak by beak, cheek to cheek, made themselves comfortable on Bruno's cigar box.

"It is now certain that the false Thomas Mann must be an agent of the Secret State Police," wrote Bruno, after he had opened his notebook again, laid it neatly on the table and bent over it like a cat with its back arched, "and I suspect he will not leave our town until we have all lost our wits. It is truly very unpleasant to think of the Nazis exploiting your good name, very highly esteemed Dr Mann, and because you, as the voice of the alternative Germany, must be careful of your reputation, I wanted to warn you—". Here Bruno suddenly stopped. He crossed out the last two sentences and began again: "Is it not terrible that the Nazis are misusing your good name? Terrible for you, Dr Mann, but also for me. Perhaps you are surprised that I write to you in German—I also speak it, but with a strong Podolian accent which unfortunately shows where I come from only too soon—and of course my love of the German language has to do with you, and also the poems and books of Rilke, Joseph Roth and Franz Kafka, whose fine and mysterious novel *The Trial* I and my former and long-forgotten fiancée translated into Polish. During the war—and hardly any of my literary Polish friends know this, not even Gombrowicz—I spent many months in Vienna, where I studied architecture without much interest, preferring to sit and read in the great libraries. The flexible rules of the *Mishnah*, the almost inspired melancholy of the Preacher, the gentle clarity of the *Shulchan Aruch*? No, those were never in my line. I long, rather, with Malte Laurids Brigge and Gustav von Aschenbach, for an end that awaits us all, but whose beauty and moment in time we should be able to determine ourselves—because God may have a plan for us, but he leaves making it until the last minute. And that is why I am so angry with your double, and his superiors in Berlin who have sent him to us. These people act as if they knew what will happen tomorrow. What shocking presumption!"

As he wrote this sentence, Bruno began sweating even more. He tore open his shirt, buttons flew across the table like shots, and Theo and Hermann, beating their wings, avoided them and then settled again on the cigar box, which was now covered with their white droppings. Bruno carefully removed the pages he had written in the last few hours from his notebook; from the drawer of Papa's desk he took a manuscript and an envelope, which already bore an address in Zürich and a stamp, and put the manuscript into it. He skimmed the letter, nodding with satisfaction several times, smiling and stroking his cheeks, and then he added a few last sentences. He wished Thomas Mann great success with the last volume of his story of *Joseph and his Brothers*, and asked him to read his, Bruno's own story, *The Homecoming*, the first that he had written in German, and on this occasion he was permitting himself to send it to the great writer. "For many years, dear Dr Mann," he concluded, "I have wished my books to appear in other countries as well, and perhaps you will like my story and see a way of helping me. Polish is a beautiful but very exclusive language, where you can choke as if on a single melon seed if you are not careful. I know what you are thinking now! No, I do not believe there is any point in waiting until even more Germans follow your double to these parts. I hope they will not come at all, and any who do come will certainly not be lovers of literature. Thank you, highly esteemed Dr Mann, for taking the time to read my letter, although you certainly have more important things to do. You have no idea how much your attention means to me. With the greatest respect, your very sad and very devoted Bruno Schulz."

Bruno put the letter in the envelope and sealed it. He got to his feet, went over to the little mirror with the white frame that hung beside the door, its paint peeling off, for a while he looked at his attractive, clever, triangular face, which suddenly seemed to him as gray as old newspaper, he tapped the tips of his big sail-like ears two or three times, and smiled at himself, and then—because the heat in his belly was intolerable by now—he slowly began removing his last items of clothing. When he was entirely naked, he shooed Theo and Hermann off the dirty cigar box again and put it, shaking his head, in the bottom drawer of the desk. Then he picked up the envelope and told the two of them, who had settled in front of the door, "Come along, children, Mrs Jakubowicz is waiting for us!" He took the thick envelope between his teeth, growled impatiently, put out the light and fell on his knees. After he had opened the door he crawled on all fours, as quietly as possible, to the ground floor and then—passing the door of Hania's apartment, behind which there was loud argument, and the sound of furniture and china being thrown around—out into Florianska Street, where only a single street lamp was on. The other lights were just going out again with a faint flickering.

Theo and Hermann and the other doves obediently followed Bruno, tripping and whirring in the air all the time, and some of the birds were already waiting for him, on the icy pavement and in the black trees in front of the building. As he slowly set off towards the school—to reach the large, dark building of the Jagiełło High School, he had to crawl to Piłsudski Street and turn off when he came to the town park—all the doves rose into the air, which was much too warm for winter, at the same time and circled around him, half human, half animal, in ellipses large and small in the silvery dark. The soft, gentle beating of their spread wings calmed Bruno, and he imagined himself following them into the many-branching starry firmament of the heavens.

But after several hundred meters, Bruno suddenly caught sight of a blaze of red firelight over the nocturnal city, he heard the sound of motor engines and loud orders, and when he looked to left or right he always saw, at the end of every alley, a gigantic, black, prehistoric insect running past on feet that rattled like tank tracks.

What's that? he thought.

No answer came.

What's that?

That is the army of Abimelech, Fear finally replied; it has come to destroy all who first made him king and remembered, only later, that he had murdered seventy of their brothers.

Oh, I see, said Bruno, of course, and he was very glad that Fear was finally talking to him again. Then he crawled on, thinking: I want Helena to start by putting the black Columbine mask on me, and tying my arms together behind my back with the Easter whips, and the rest is up to her. Although he had been on the move for almost an hour, he had only just reached the portico of the town park, he was breathing heavily, his knees were sore and bloody and the doves in the sky above Drohobycz flew one after another into the red firelight, where they burned like tinder.

TWO STORIES
BY BRUNO SCHULZ

BRUNO SCHULZ was a Polish-Jewish writer and artist. Born in 1892 in Drohobycz, Poland (now part of Ukraine), he worked for many years as an art teacher in his hometown. He published two collections of short fiction, *The Street of Crocodiles* and *Sanatorium Under the Sign of the Hourglass*. In 1942 he was killed by a Gestapo officer and much of his work, including a novel titled *The Messiah*, was lost. The little that remains has influenced numerous important writers, including J. M. Coetzee, Philip Roth, Cynthia Ozick, Salman Rushdie, David Grossman and Jonathan Safran Foer.

'Schulz was incomparably gifted as an
explorer of his own inner life'
J. M. COETZEE

'A man of enormous artistic gifts
and imaginative riches'
PHILIP ROTH

'Bruno Schulz was one of the great writers, one of
the great transmogrifiers of the world into words'
JOHN UPDIKE

'I read Schulz's stories and felt the gush of life'
DAVID GROSSMAN

BIRDS

C AME THE YELLOW DAYS OF winter, filled with boredom. The rust-colored earth was covered with a threadbare, meager tablecloth of snow full of holes. There was not enough of it for some of the roofs and so they stood there, black and brown, shingle and thatch, arks containing the sooty expanses of attics— coal black cathedrals, bristling with ribs of rafters, beams, and spars—the dark lungs of winter winds. Each dawn revealed new chimney stacks and chimney pots which had emerged during the hours of darkness, blown up by the night winds: the black pipes of a devil's organ. The chimney sweeps could not get rid of the crows which in the evening covered the branches of the trees around the church with living black leaves, then took off, fluttering, and came back, each clinging to its own place on its own branch, only to fly away at dawn in large flocks, like gusts of soot, flakes of dirt, undulating and fantastic, blackening with their insistent cawing the musty yellow streaks of light. The days hardened with cold and boredom like last year's loaves of bread. One began to cut them with blunt knives without appetite, with a lazy indifference.

Father had stopped going out. He banked up the stoves, studied the ever-elusive essence of fire, experienced the salty, metallic taste and the smoky smell of wintry salamanders that licked the shiny soot in the throat of the chimney. He applied himself lovingly at that time to all manner of small repairs in the upper regions of the rooms. At all hours of the day one could see him crouched on top of a ladder, working at something under the ceiling, at the cornices over the tall windows, at the counterweights and chains of the hanging lamps. Following the custom of house painters, he used a pair of steps as enormous stilts and he felt perfectly happy in that bird's-eye perspective close to the sky, leaves and birds painted on the ceiling. He grew more and more remote from practical affairs. When my mother, worried and unhappy about his condition, tried to draw him into a conversation about business, about the payments due at the end of the month, he listened to her absentmindedly, anxiety showing in his abstracted look. Sometimes he stopped her with a warning gesture of the hand in order to run to a corner of the room, put his ear to a crack in the floor and, by lifting the index fingers of both hands, emphasize the gravity of the investigation, and begin to listen intently. At that time we did not yet understand the sad origin of these eccentricities, the deplorable complex which had been maturing in him.

Mother had no influence over him, but he gave a lot of respectful attention to Adela. The cleaning of his room was to him a great and important ceremony, of which he always arranged to be a witness, watching all Adela's movements with a mixture of apprehension and pleasurable excitement. He ascribed to all her functions a deeper, symbolic meaning. When, with young firm gestures, the girl pushed a long-handled broom along the floor, Father could hardly bear it. Tears would stream from his eyes, silent laughter transformed his face, and his body was shaken by spasms of delight. He was ticklish to the point of madness. It was enough for Adela to waggle her fingers at him to imitate tickling, for him to rush through all the rooms in a wild panic, banging the doors after him, to fall at last on the bed in the farthest room and wriggle in convulsions of laughter, imagining the tickling which he found irresistible. Because of this, Adela's power over Father was almost limitless.

At that time we noticed for the first time Father's passionate interest in animals. To begin with, it was the passion of the huntsman and the artist rolled into one. It was also perhaps a deeper, biological sympathy of one creature for kindred, yet different, forms of life, a kind of experimenting in the unexplored regions of existence. Only at a later stage did matters take that uncanny, complicated, essentially sinful and unnatural turn, which it is better not to bring into the light of day.

But it all began with the hatching out of birds' eggs.

With a great outlay of effort and money, Father imported from Hamburg, or Holland, or from zoo-logical stations in Africa, birds' eggs on which he set enormous brood hens from Belgium. It was a process which fascinated me as well—this hatching out of the chicks, which were real anomalies of shape and color. It was difficult to anticipate—in these monsters with enormous, fantastic beaks which they opened wide immediately after birth, hissing greedily to show the backs of their throats, in these lizards with frail, naked bodies of hunchbacks—the future peacocks, pheasants, grouse, or condors. Placed in cotton wool, in baskets, this dragon brood lifted blind, walleyed heads on thin necks, croaking voicelessly from their dumb throats. My father would walk along the shelves, dressed in a green baize apron, like a gardener in a hothouse of cacti, and conjure up from nothingness these blind bubbles, pulsating with life, these impotent bellies receiving the outside world only in the form of food, these growths on the surface of life, climbing blindfolded toward the light. A few weeks later, when these blind buds of matter burst open, the rooms were filled with the bright chatter and scintillating chirruping of their new inhabitants. The birds perched on the curtain pelmets, on the tops of wardrobes; they nestled in the tangle of tin branches and the metal scrolls of the hanging lamps.

While Father pored over his large ornithological textbooks and studied their colored plates, these feathery phantasms seemed to rise from the pages and fill the rooms with colors, with splashes of crimson, strips of sapphire, verdigris, and silver. At feeding time they formed a motley, undulating bed on the floor, a living carpet which at the intrusion of a stranger would fall apart, scatter into fragments, flutter in the air, and finally settle high under the ceilings. I remember in particular a certain condor, an enormous bird with a featherless neck, its face wrinkled and knobbly. It was an emaciated ascetic, a Buddhist lama, full of imperturbable dignity in its behavior, guided by the rigid ceremonial of its great species. When it sat facing my father, motionless in the monumental position of ageless Egyptian idols, its eyes covered with a whitish cataract which it pulled down sideways over its pupil to shut itself up completely in the contemplation of its dignified solitude—it seemed, with its stony profile, like an older brother of my father's. Its body and muscles seemed to be made of the same material, it had the same hard, wrinkled skin, the same desiccated bony face, the same horny, deep eye sockets. Even the hands, strong in the joints, my father's long, thick hands with their rounded nails, had their counterpart in the condor's claws. I could not resist the impression, when looking at the sleeping condor, that I was in the presence of a mummy—a dried-out, shrunken mummy of my father. I believe that even my mother noticed this strange resemblance, although we never discussed the subject. It is significant that the condor used my father's chamber pot.

Not content with the hatching out of more and more new specimens, my father arranged the marriages of birds in the attic, he sent out matchmakers, he tied up eager attractive birds in the holes and crannies under the roof, and soon the roof of our house, an enormous double-rigged shingle roof, became a real birds' hostel, a Noah's ark to which all kinds of feathery creatures flew from far afield. Long after the liquidation of the birds' paradise, this tradition persisted in the avian world and during the period of spring migration our roof was besieged by whole flocks of cranes, pelicans, peacocks, and sundry other birds. However, after a short period of splendor, the whole undertaking took a sorry turn.

It soon became necessary to move my father to two rooms at the top of the house which had served as storage rooms. We could hear from there, at dawn, the mixed clangor of birds' voices. The wooden walls of the attic rooms, helped by the resonance of the empty space under the gables, sounded with the roar, the flutterings, the crowing, the gurgling, the mating cries. For a few weeks Father was lost to view. He only rarely came down to the apartment and, when he did, we noticed that he seemed to have shrunk, to have become smaller and thinner. Occasionally forgetting himself, he would rise from his chair at table, wave his arms as if they were wings, and emit a long-drawn-out bird's call while his eyes misted over. Then, rather embarrassed, he would join us in laughing it off and try to turn the whole incident into a joke.

One day, during spring cleaning, Adela suddenly appeared in Father's bird kingdom. Stopping in the doorway, she wrung her hands at the fetid smell that filled the room, the heaps of droppings covering the floor, the tables, and the chairs. Without hesitation, she flung open the window and, with the help of a long broom, she prodded the whole mass of birds into life. A fiendish cloud of feathers and wings arose screaming, and Adela, like a furious maenad protected by the whirlwind of her thyrsus, danced the dance of destruction. My father, waving his arms in panic, tried to lift himself into the air with his feathered flock. Slowly the winged cloud thinned until at last Adela remained on the battlefield, exhausted and out of breath, along with my father, who now, adopting a worried hangdog expression, was ready to accept complete defeat.

A moment later, my father came downstairs—a broken man, an exiled king who had lost his throne and his kingdom.

CINNAMON SHOPS

A T THE TIME OF THE shortest, sleepy winter days, edged on both sides with the furry dusk of mornings and evenings, when the city reached out deeper and deeper into the labyrinth of winter nights, and was shaken reluctantly into consciousness by the short dawn, my father was already lost, sold and surrendered to the other sphere.

His face and head became overgrown with a wild and recalcitrant shock of gray hair, bristling in irregular tufts and spikes, shooting out from warts, from his eyebrows, from the openings of his nostrils and giving him the appearance of an old ill-tempered fox.

His sense of smell and his hearing sharpened extraordinarily and one could see from the expression of his tense silent face that through the intermediary of these two senses he remained in permanent contact with the unseen world of mouse holes, dark corners, chimney vents, and dusty spaces under the floor.

He was a vigilant and attentive observer, a prying fellow conspirator, of the rustlings, the nightly creakings, the secret gnawing life of the floor. He was so engrossed in it that he became completely submerged in an inaccessible sphere and one which he did not even attempt to discuss with us.

He often used to flip his fingers and laugh softly to himself when the manifestations of the unseen became too absurd; he then exchanged knowing looks with our cat, which, also initiated in these mysteries, would lift its cynical cold striped face, closing the slanting chinks of its eyes with an air of indifference and boredom.

It sometimes happened that, during a meal, my father would suddenly put aside his knife and fork and, with his napkin still tied around his neck, would rise from the table with a feline movement, tiptoe to the door of the adjoining room, and peer through the keyhole with the utmost caution. Then, with a bashful smile, he would return to the table slightly embarrassed, murmuring and whispering indistinctly in tune with the interior monologue that wholly preoccupied him.

To provide some distraction for him and to tear him away from these morbid speculations, my mother would force him to go out for a walk in the evenings. He went in silence, without protest but also without enthusiasm, distrait and absent in spirit. Once we even went all together to the theater.

We found ourselves again in that large, badly lit, dirty hall, full of somnolent human chatter and aimless confusion. But when we had made our way through the crowd, there emerged before us an enormous pale blue curtain, like the sky of another firmament. Large painted pink masks with puffed-up cheeks floated in a huge expanse of canvas. The artificial sky spread out in both directions, swelling with the powerful breath of pathos and of great gestures, with the atmosphere of that fictitious floodlit world created on the echoing scaffolding of the stage. The tremor sailing across the large area of that sky, the breath of the vast canvas which made the masks revive and grow, revealed the illusory character of that firmament, caused that vibration of reality which, in metaphysical moments, we experience as the glimmer of revelation.

The masks fluttered their red eyelids, their colored lips whispered voicelessly, and I knew that the moment was imminent when the tension of mystery would reach its zenith and the swollen skies of the curtain would really burst open to reveal incredible and dazzling events.

But I was not allowed to experience that moment, because in the meantime my father had begun to betray a certain anxiety. He was feeling in all his pockets and at last declared that he had left behind at home a wallet containing money and certain most important documents.

After a short conference with my father, during which Adela's honesty was submitted to a hasty assessment, it was suggested that I should go home to look for the wallet. According to my mother, there was still plenty of time before the curtain rose, and, fleet-footed as I was, I had every chance of returning in time.

I stepped into a winter night bright from the illuminations of the sky. It was one of those clear nights when the starry firmament is so wide and spreads so far that it seems to be divided and broken up into a mass of separate skies, sufficient for a whole month of winter nights and providing silver and painted globes to cover all the nightly phenomena, adventures, occurrences, and carnivals.

It is exceedingly thoughtless to send a young boy out on an urgent and important errand into a night like that, because in its semi-obscurity the streets multiply, becoming confused and interchanged. There open up, deep inside a city, reflected streets, streets which are doubles, make-believe streets. One's imagination, bewitched and misled, creates illusory maps of the apparently familiar districts, maps in which streets have their proper places and usual names but are provided with new and fictitious configurations by the inexhaustible inventiveness of the night. The temptations of such winter nights begin usually with the innocent desire to take a shortcut, to use a quicker but less familiar way. Attractive possibilities arise of shortening a complicated walk by taking some never-used side street. But on that occasion things began differently.

Having taken a few steps, I realized that I was not wearing my overcoat. I wanted to turn back, but after a moment that seemed to me an unnecessary waste of time, especially as the night was not cold at all; on the contrary, I could feel waves of an unseasonal warmth, like breezes of a spring night. The snow shrank into a white fluff, into a harmless fleece smelling sweetly of violets. Similar white fluffs were sailing across the sky on which the moon was doubled and trebled, showing all its phases and positions at once.

On that night the sky laid bare its internal construction in many sections, which, like quasi-anatomical exhibits, showed the spirals and whorls of light, the pale green solids of darkness, the plasma of space, the tissue of dreams.

On such a night, it was impossible to walk along Rampart Street, or any other of the dark streets which are the obverse, the lining as it were, of the four sides of Market Square, and not to remember that at that late hour the strange and most attractive shops were sometimes open, the shops which on ordinary days one tended to overlook. I used to call them cinnamon shops because of the dark paneling of their walls.

These truly noble shops, open late at night, have always been the objects of my ardent interest. Dimly lit, their dark and solemn interiors were redolent of the smell of paint, varnish, and incense; of the aroma of distant countries and rare commodities. You could find in them Bengal lights, magic boxes, the stamps of long-forgotten countries, Chinese decals, indigo, calaphony from Malabar, the eggs of exotic insects, parrots, toucans, live salamanders and basilisks, mandrake roots, mechanical toys from Nuremberg, homunculi in jars, microscopes, binoculars, and, most especially, strange and rare books, old folio volumes full of astonishing engravings and amazing stories.

I remember those old dignified merchants who served their customers with downcast eyes, in discreet silence, and who were full of wisdom and tolerance for their customers' most secret whims. But most of all, I remember a bookshop in which I once glanced at some rare and forbidden pamphlets, the publications of secret societies lifting the veil on tantalizing and unknown mysteries.

I so rarely had the occasion to visit these shops—especially with a small but sufficient amount of money in my pocket—that I could not forgo the opportunity I had now, in spite of the important mission entrusted to me.

According to my calculations I ought to turn into a narrow lane and pass two or three side streets in order to reach the street of the night shops. This would take me even farther from home, but by cutting across Saltworks Street I could make good the delay.

Lent wings by my desire to visit the cinnamon shops, I turned into a street I knew and ran rather than walked, anxious not to lose my way. I passed three or four streets, but still there was no sign of the turning I wanted. What is more, the appearance of the street was different from what I had expected. Nor was there any sign of the shops. I was in a street of houses with no doors and whose tightly shut windows were blind from reflected moonlight. On the other side of those houses—I thought—must run the street from which they were accessible. I was walking faster now, rather disturbed, beginning to give up the idea of visiting the cinnamon shops. All I wanted now was to get out of there quickly into some part of the city I knew better. I reached the end of the street, unsure where it would lead me. I found myself in a broad, sparsely built-up avenue, very long and straight. I felt on me the breath of a wide-open space. Close to the pavement or in the midst of their gardens, picturesque villas stood there, the private houses of the rich. In the gaps between them were parks and walls of orchards. The whole area looked like Lesznianska Street in its lower and rarely visited part. The moonlight filtered through a thousand feathery clouds, like silver scales on the sky. It was pale and bright as daylight—only the parks and gardens stood black in that silvery landscape.

Looking more closely at one of the buildings, I realized that what I saw was the back of the high school, which I had never seen from that side. I was just approaching the gate which, to my surprise, was open; the entrance hall was lit. I walked in and found myself on the red carpet of the passage. I hoped to be able to slip through unobserved and come out through the front gate, thus taking a splendid shortcut.

I remembered that at that late hour there might be, in Professor Arendt's classroom, one of the voluntary classes which in winter were always held in the late evenings and to which we all flocked, fired by the enthusiasm for art which that excellent teacher had awakened in us.

A small group of industrious pupils was almost lost in the large dark hall on whose walls the enormous shadows of our heads broke abruptly, thrown by the light of two small candles set in bottles.

To be truthful, we did not draw very much during these classes and the professor was not very exacting. Some boys brought cushions from home and stretched themselves out on benches for a short nap. Only the most diligent of us gathered around the candle, in the golden circle of its light.

We usually had to wait a long while for the professor's arrival, filling the time with sleepy conversation. At last the door from his room would open and he would enter—short, bearded, given to esoteric smiles and discreet silences and exuding an aroma of secrecy.

He shut the door of his study carefully behind him: through it for a brief moment we could see over his head a crowd of plaster shadows, the classical fragments of suffering. Niobides, Danaïdes, and Tantalides, the whole sad and sterile Olympus, wilting for years on end in that plaster-cast museum. The light in his room was opaque even in daytime, thick from the dreams of plaster-cast heads, from empty looks, ashen profiles, and meditations dissolving into nothingness. We liked to listen sometimes in front of that door—listen to the silence laden with the sighs and whispers of the crumbling gods withering in the boredom and monotony of their twilight.

The professor walked with great dignity and unction up and down among the half-empty benches on which, in small groups, we were drawing amidst the gray reflections of a winter night. Everything was quiet and cozy. Some of my classmates were asleep. The candles were burning low in their bottles. The professor delved into a deep bookcase, full of old folios, unfashionable engravings, woodcuts, and prints. He showed us, with his esoteric gestures, old lithographs of night landscapes, of tree clumps in moonlight, of avenues in wintry parks outlined black on the white moonlit background.

Amid sleepy talk, time passed unnoticed. It ran by unevenly, as if making knots in the passage of hours, swallowing somewhere whole empty periods. Without transition, our whole gang found ourselves on the way home long after midnight on the garden path white with snow, flanked by the black, dry thicket of bushes. We walked alongside that hairy rim of darkness, brushing against the furry bushes, their lower branches snapping under our feet in the bright night, in a false milky brightness. The diffuse whiteness of light filtered by the snow, by the pale air, by the milky space, was like the gray paper of an engraving on which the thick bushes corresponded to the deep black lines of decoration. The night was copying now, at that late hour, the nightly landscapes of Professor Arendt's engravings, re-enacting his fantasies.

In the black thickets of the park, in the hairy coat of bushes, in the mass of crusty twigs there were nooks, niches, nests of deepest fluffy blackness, full of confusion, secret gestures, conniving looks. It was warm and quiet there. We sat on the soft snow in our heavy coats, cracking hazelnuts of which there was a profusion in that springlike winter. Through the copse, weasels wandered silently, martens and ichneumons, furry, ferreting elongated animals on short legs, stinking of sheepskin. We suspected that among them were the exhibits from the school cabinets which, although degutted and molting, felt on that white night in their empty bowels the voice of the eternal instinct, the mating urge, and returned to the thickets for short moments of illusory life.

But slowly the phosphorescence of the springlike snow became dulled: it vanished then, giving way to a thick black darkness preceding dawn. Some of us fell asleep in the warm snow, others went groping in the dark for the doors of their houses and walked blindly into the sleep of their parents and brothers, into a continuation of deep snoring which caught up with them on their late return.

These nightly drawing sessions held a secret charm for me, so that now I could not forgo the opportunity of looking for a moment into the art room. I decided, however, that I would not stop for more than a little while. But walking up the back stairs, their cedar wood resounding under my steps, I realized that I was in a wing of the school building completely unknown to me.

Not even a murmur interrupted the solemn silence. The passages were broader in this wing, covered with a thick carpet and most elegant. Small, darkly glowing lamps were hung at each corner. Turning the first of these, I found myself in an even wider, more sumptuous hall. In one of its walls there was a wide glass arcade leading to the interior of an apartment. I could see a long enfilade of rooms, furnished with great magnificence. The eye wandered over silk hangings, gilded mirrors, costly furniture, and crystal chandeliers and into the velvety softness of the luxurious interiors, shimmering with lights, entangled garlands, and budding flowers. The profound stillness of these empty rooms was filled with the secret glances exchanged by mirrors and the panic of friezes running high along the walls and disappearing into the stucco of the white ceilings.

I faced all that magnificence with admiration and awe, guessing that my nightly escapade had brought me unexpectedly into the headmaster's wing, to his private apartment. I stood there with a beating heart, rooted to the spot by curiosity, ready to escape at the slightest noise. How would I justify, if surprised, that nocturnal visit, that impudent prying? In one of those deep plush armchairs there might sit, unobserved and still, the young daughter of the headmaster. She might lift her eyes to mine— black, sibylline, quiet eyes, the gaze of which none could hold. But to retreat halfway, not having carried through the plan I had, would be cowardly. Besides, deep silence reigned in those magnificent interiors, lit by the hazy light of an undefined hour. Through the arcades of the passage, I saw on the far side of the living room a large glass door leading to the terrace. It was so still everywhere that I felt suddenly emboldened. It did not strike me as too risky to walk down the short steps leading to the level of the living room, to take a few quick steps across the large, costly carpet and to find myself on the terrace from which I could get back without any difficulty to the familiar street.

This is what I did. When I found myself on the parquet floor under the potted palms that reached up to the frieze of the ceiling, I noticed that now I really was on neutral ground, because the living room did not have a front wall. It was a kind of large loggia, connected by a few steps with a city square, an enclosed part of the square, because some of the garden furniture stood directly on the pavement. I ran down the short flight of stone steps and found myself at street level once more.

The constellations in the sky stood steeply on their heads, all the stars had made an about-turn, but the moon, buried under the featherbed of clouds which were lit by its unseen presence, seemed still to have before her an endless journey and, absorbed in her complicated heavenly procedures, did not think of dawn.

A few horse-drawn cabs loomed black in the street, half-broken and loose jointed like crippled, dozing crabs or cockroaches. A driver leaned down toward me from his high box. He had a small red kindly face. "Shall we go, master?" he asked. The cab shook in all the joints and ligatures of its many-limbed body and made a start on its light wheels.

But who would entrust oneself on such a night to the whims of an unpredictable cabby? Amid the click of the axles, amid the thud of the box and the roof, I could not agree with him on my destination. He nodded indulgently at everything I said and sang to himself. We drove in a circle around the city.

In front of an inn stood a group of cabbies who waved friendly hands to him. He answered gaily and then, without stopping the carriage, he threw the reins on my knees, jumped down from the box, and joined the group of his colleagues. The horse, an old wise cab horse, looked round cursorily and went on in a monotonous regular trot. In fact, that horse inspired confidence—it seemed smarter than its driver. But I myself could not drive, so I had to rely on the horse's will. We turned into a suburban street, bordered on both sides by gardens. As we advanced, these gardens slowly changed into parks with tall trees and the parks in turn into forests.

I shall never forget that luminous journey on that brightest of winter nights. The colored map of the heavens expanded into an immense dome, on which there loomed fantastic lands, oceans and seas, marked with the lines of stellar currents and eddies, with the brilliant streaks of heavenly geography. The air became light to breathe and shimmered like silver gauze. One could smell violets. From under the white woolly lamb-skin of snow, trembling anemones appeared with a speck of moonlight in each delicate cup. The whole forest seemed to be illuminated by thousands of lights and by the stars falling in profusion from the December sky. The air pulsated with a secret spring, with the matchless purity of snow and violets. We entered a hilly landscape. The lines of hills, bristling with the bare spikes of trees, rose like sighs of bliss. I saw on these happy slopes groups of wanderers, gathering among the moss and the bushes the fallen stars which now were damp from snow. The road became steep, the horse began to slip on it and pulled the creaking cab only with an effort. I was happy. My lungs soaked up the blissful spring in the air, the freshness of snow and stars. Before the horse's breast the rampart of white snowy foam grew higher and higher, and it could hardly wade through that pure fresh mass. At last we stopped. I got out of the cab. The horse was panting, hanging its head. I hugged its head to my breast and saw that there were tears in its large eyes. I noticed a round black wound on its belly. "Why did not you tell me?" I whispered, crying. "My dearest, I did it for you," the horse said and became very small, like a wooden toy. I left him and felt wonderfully light and happy. I was debating whether to wait for the small local train which passed through here or to walk back to the city. I began to walk down a steep path, winding like a serpent amid the forest; at first in a light elastic step; later, passing into a brisk happy run which became gradually faster, until it resembled a gliding descent on skis. I could regulate my speed at will and change course by light movements of my body.

On the outskirts of the city, I slowed this triumphal run and changed it into a sedate walk. The moon still rode high in the sky. The transformations of the sky, the metamorphoses of its multiple domes into more and more complicated configurations were endless. Like a silver astrolabe the sky disclosed on that magic night its internal mechanism and showed in infinite evolutions the mathematics of its cogs and wheels.

In Market Square I met some people enjoying a walk. All of them, enchanted by the displays of that night, walked with uplifted faces, silvery from the magic of the sky. I completely stopped worrying about Father's wallet. My father, absorbed by his manias, had probably forgotten its loss by now, and as for my mother, I did not much care.

On such a night, unique in the year, one has happy thoughts and inspirations, one feels touched by the divine finger of poetry. Full of ideas and projects, I wanted to walk toward my home, but met some school friends with books under their arms. They were on their way to school already, having been wakened by the brightness of that night that would not end.

We went for a walk all together along a steeply falling street, pervaded by the scent of violets; uncertain whether it was the magic of the night which lay like silver on the snow or whether it was the light of dawn…

PUSHKIN PRESS

Pushkin Press was founded in 1997, and publishes novels, essays, memoirs, children's books—everything from timeless classics to the urgent and contemporary.

This book is part of the Pushkin Collection of paperbacks, designed to be as satisfying as possible to hold and to enjoy. It is typeset in Monotype Baskerville, based on the transitional English serif typeface designed in the mid-eighteenth century by John Baskerville. It was litho-printed on Munken Premium White Paper and notch-bound by the independently owned printer TJ International in Padstow, Cornwall. The cover, with French flaps, was printed on Colorplan Pristine White paper. The paper and cover board are both acid-free and Forest Stewardship Council (FSC) certified.

Pushkin Press publishes the best writing from around the world—great stories, beautifully produced, to be read and read again.

STEFAN ZWEIG · EDGAR ALLAN POE · ISAAC BABEL
TOMÁS GONZÁLEZ · ULRICH PLENZDORF · TEFFI
VELIBOR ČOLIĆ · LOUISE DE VILMORIN · MARCEL AYMÉ
ALEXANDER PUSHKIN · MAXIM BILLER · JULIEN GRACQ
BROTHERS GRIMM · HUGO VON HOFMANNSTHAL
GEORGE SAND · PHILIPPE BEAUSSANT · IVÁN REPILA
E.T.A. HOFFMANN · ALEXANDER LERNET-HOLENIA
YASUSHI INOUE · HENRY JAMES · FRIEDRICH TORBERG
ARTHUR SCHNITZLER · ANTOINE DE SAINT-EXUPÉRY
MACHI TAWARA · GAITO GAZDANOV · HERMANN HESSE
LOUIS COUPERUS · JAN JACOB SLAUERHOFF
PAUL MORAND · MARK TWAIN · PAUL FOURNEL
ANTAL SZERB · JONA OBERSKI · MEDARDO FRAILE
HÉCTOR ABAD · PETER HANDKE · ERNST WEISS
PENELOPE DELTA · RAYMOND RADIGUET · PETR KRÁL
ITALO SVEVO · RÉGIS DEBRAY · BRUNO SCHULZ